Codebreakers

by

Deborah Chancellor

Illustrated by Zoografic

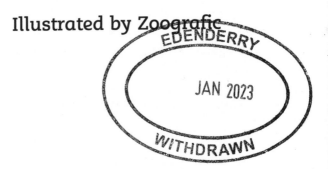

For Matthew

First published in 2009 in Great Britain by
Barrington Stoke Ltd
18 Walker Street, Edinburgh, EH3 7LP

www.barringtonstoke.co.uk

ISBN: 978-1-84299-611-9

Printed in Great Britain by Bell & Bain Ltd

Contents

Chapter 1
Bad Day

Nobody wants to know about my life, so what's the point of writing a blog? I used to think blogs were the biggest waste of time. But I don't think that any more. Now I reckon that writing down what happens to you helps you make sense of it all. Maybe it's like cracking a code to read a hidden message.

Let me explain about codes. I'm crazy about them. I love the fact that they're a kind of secret language, which only you and one other person can understand. It's like you're both floating above the ground in a bubble, but at any moment your bubble might burst. If your code is cracked, you'll come crashing down to Earth.

My friend Jack is into codes, just like me. We spend hours inventing codes for each other, and even longer trying to break them. We keep a hand-book about codes. It's called Harry and Jack's Code Hand-book. It's top secret, of course.

You could say that codes got Jack and me into trouble, but they saved us, too.

****

Last Sunday started off just like any other ordinary day. It was raining, so in the afternoon Jack and I thought we'd go and see a film. There isn't a cinema where we live, so we had to catch a train to Harlow, a town nearby.

At the station, the waiting room was full of people trying to keep out of the rain. I saw a man on a bench in the corner, hunched over his mobile phone. He was jabbing away at the keypad. He frowned and bit his lip. He was going red in the face and looked very angry. I gave Jack a nudge.

"What's up with him?" I said, looking at the man.

"Having a bad day, I suppose, Harry," said Jack.

The fast train for London pulled into the platform. The man grabbed his bag and left the waiting room. We watched as he ran onto the train, the doors beeping as they closed behind him. Suddenly, he began to search his pockets for something. He turned to the window and started to bang his fist on the glass as the train moved away.

"He's left his phone behind!" said Jack. It had fallen under the bench where the man had been sitting. I went over to pick it up.

"It's brand new," I said.

Jack took the phone and began to play around with it and to fiddle with the buttons.

"That's odd," he said. "Take a look at these texts."

"You can't read his texts, they're private!" I said. I was shocked. Jack grinned.

"You're dead right there," he replied. "Top secret, more like!"

The text message on the phone was a jumble of letters. They were in capitals, all the words were the same length, and there were no commas or full stops.

I looked at Jack. He didn't say a word, but I knew what he was thinking.

"It's in code!" we both said together.

We found the inbox and began to scroll through the other texts. Just like the first one, they were all in some kind of code.

What had we stumbled upon?

Code Hand-book

Writing Codes

A message in code is called 'codetext' or 'ciphertext'. Most often, it is written in CAPITAL LETTERS.

A decoded message is called 'plaintext'. It tends to be written in lower case letters.

When you write a message in codetext, keep it short. Don't use commas or full stops, and don't repeat any words, because this will give clues to a code breaker.

Make all the 'words' in your codetext about the same length - five or six letters long. This makes the message harder to decode.

Chapter 2
Lost Property

"I think we'd better hand the phone in," I said. "There's something strange about all this. Why would anyone want to send texts in code?"

"Why not?" said Jack. "It's more cool that way. Perhaps that man on the train was a secret agent."

"Yeah, right," I said. "He crashed his Aston Martin and was forced to travel on public transport ..." Jack laughed.

We went into the ticket office, but there was no one there to ask about lost property.

"It's Sunday," I said. "Everyone's gone home early."

"We might as well do the same," said Jack, looking up at the screen that showed the train times. "Our train's been cancelled. It's a good job we've got something else to do now. Let's go back to my place, Harry, and crack those codes."

"Do you think we should?" I said, but Jack rolled his eyes.

"Chill out!" he sighed. "We can bring the phone back here tomorrow, but let's have some fun with it before we do."

****

"Make yourself at home," grinned Jack, sitting down at the desk in his bedroom. The floor was littered with books, papers and half-eaten snacks, so this wasn't easy. As I looked around for somewhere to sit, there was a loud bleep. It was the mobile phone.

"Another text!" said Jack, flipping open the phone. "Come on, Harry, we've got work to do!"

I started reading out the text messages. Jack wrote them down, taking his time so he didn't make a mistake.

"If we get one letter wrong it will mess it all up," he said.

When Jack had written down the last message, he stood up and frowned.

"There's got to be some kind of pattern. We could start by working out which letters come up most often. That might tell us which letters stand for vowels, and other common letters in English."

"What if the code isn't in English?" I asked.

Jack glared at me. "Why do you always look for problems?" he snapped.

Angry with Jack, I picked up our Code Hand-book and flicked through it for a while. Perhaps that would give us some ideas. But when I looked up, Jack was holding his head in his hands.

"My head hurts," he said.

"Listen, Jack ..." I began. But Jack stopped me.

"We can't do this, it's too hard. Let's just forget it. I'll see you in the morning, and we'll drop the phone off on the way to school."

I felt annoyed with Jack for giving up so quickly. I knew we could crack the code, but it would take two of us to do it – I couldn't do it alone.

Code Hand-book

Instant Codes

Type a message on a computer, click on it and select a symbol font, such as Wingdings. At the click of a mouse, your 'plaintext' becomes 'codetext'. For example:

'I didn't know that' would change into:

♚   ♎♓♎■⊠♦   &■□♦   ♦♒♋♦

The most common letter in English is 'e'. It occurs 12.7% of the time, so in a message of 1,000 letters, about 127 of the letters will be 'e'. Remember this when you are cracking a code, as the most common letter in the code probably stands for 'e'.

If the letters of the alphabet are re-arranged in order of how often they are used in English, the alphabet looks like this:

e, t, a, o, i, n, s, h, r, d, l, u, c, m, w, f, y, g, p, b, v, k, x, j, q, z

Chapter 3
Late Night Call

It would have been much easier if things had ended there – it would have been safer, for sure. But this was only the beginning of the story.

I went to bed early that night. My dreams were confused. I was being chased, but I didn't know who was chasing me. My legs felt heavy, and I began to slow down. All the time, the people running after me were getting closer, while a ringing in my ears was growing louder and louder ...

At last, the ring tone of my mobile phone forced me awake. I looked at my alarm clock, surprised to see that it was only 11.30pm. I picked up the phone on my bed-side table and answered the call. It was Jack.

"Something's happened, Harry," he said. "You've got to come round here, right now!"

"Who do you think you are?" I replied, feeling irritated. "Telling me to go away this afternoon, and now asking me to come back in the middle of the night."

I was wide-awake now.

"I can't explain on the phone," said Jack. "Just take my word for it. Hurry, I haven't got long ..." Suddenly the phone went dead.

I knew this wasn't a joke. Jack did wind me up sometimes, but this wasn't one of those times. I threw on some clothes, crept down the stairs and let myself out of the back door. I got on my bike and in five minutes I was at his house. Jack was waiting for me by the front gate, standing with his bike in the shadows.

"What are you playing at?" I whispered. "Why did you hang up like that, and where are we going? It's a bit late for a trip to the park."

"That's just where we *are* going," Jack replied grimly.

"I had a call on that mobile."

"Who from? What was it about?"

"I think it was that man on the train – the one who the phone belongs to. He told me to take the phone to the park at midnight, and

leave it under the slide in the play-ground. He said if I didn't do this tonight, I'd regret it ..." Jack's voice trailed off. "Harry, he's traced the mobile phone signal, and he knows where I live."

It took me a few seconds to take all this in.

"Why didn't you phone the police?" I asked. "This is stupid, Jack. And dangerous."

"He warned me that if I grassed him up, I'd never talk again by the time he'd finished with me," Jack got on his bike.

"Come with me, Harry," he said in a low voice. "I don't want to do this on my own."

Only a few hours ago I had been wishing for adventure. Now it had come my way, I wasn't sure what to think.

"We're in this together, Jack," I said, trying to sound braver than I felt. "We'd better get going – it's almost midnight."

Code Hand-book

Hiding Codes

People work hard to hide coded messages. If a code can't be found, it can't be cracked.

A good way to hide coded messages is to write in invisible ink. People have used lemon juice and vinegar since Roman times - the writing shows up when the paper is warmed. Believe it or not, you can also use pee as invisible ink!

In ancient China, a message was sometimes written on silk, rolled into a ball and coated with wax. A messenger swallowed the wax ball and hurried to meet his friends. He went to the toilet to 'pop out' the message!

Chapter 4
The Drop-off

As we rode away from Jack's house, I was nervous about what we were about to do, but I also felt a wave of excitement wash over me. It was a dark night and there was no moon in the sky. The stars above our heads sparkled like diamonds on a black, velvet cloth.

At the park gates, we leaned our bikes against the railings. I checked my watch.

"It's three minutes to midnight," I said to Jack. "Have you got the phone?"

"Right here," replied Jack, pulling it out of his pocket. His hands were shaking.

"I forgot to bring a torch," he said, peering into the darkness beyond the park gates.

"We don't need one," I replied. "We've known this park since we were kids. We could find our way to the play-ground with our eyes shut, if we had to."

We climbed over the railings and set off across the soft, wet grass. Ahead of us, a pin-prick of light flicked on and off. It was over towards the play-ground.

"He's already there!" cried Jack, a note of panic creeping into his voice.

"We've got what he wants, haven't we?" I replied. "If we do what he says, we'll be fine."

We walked on, and soon a tall, dark shape loomed up in front of us. It was the children's slide in the play-ground.

"Put the phone down under there," I whispered. "Then run!"

Five minutes later we were back on our bikes, racing along the empty streets. The warm glow of the street-lights lifted the cloud of fear that had settled on us both. The rush of relief made us laugh out loud.

"That wasn't so bad after all!" said Jack.

"I wouldn't do it again if you paid me!" I replied, suddenly serious. "I think we should go to the police now."

"Are you off your head?" Jack cried. "He'll only leave us alone if we keep our mouths shut."

We reached Jack's house. "Anyway," Jack went on. "Don't you want to know what this is all about? If we tell the police now, we'll spend all night at the police station. We'll have to waste time trying to explain what happened, while we could be cracking those codes."

"I thought you'd given up on them!" I said.

"Not any more," replied Jack. "The coded texts hold the key to all this. It's a good job we wrote them all down. That man wanted his phone back because he didn't want anyone to decode the texts. He thinks he's in the clear now. But we're going to crack those codes and work out what he's up to before it's too late."

I had to admit Jack had a point.

"Well, we've only got about six hours to do this," I said. "I'm going to have to get home before it gets light, and Mum finds out I'm missing. She'll go mad."

"There's nothing like working against the clock," grinned Jack.

We parked our bikes in Jack's garden and slipped into his house.

It was going to be a long night.

Code Hand-book

Important Codes

In the First World War, Germany wanted to make Mexico attack America. Germany's plans were found out in 1917, when the Allies decoded a top-secret German telegram. After that, the Americans made up their minds to join the war against Germany.

In World War Two, a team of brilliant code breakers cracked the German 'Enigma' code. This meant that the Allies could understand their enemy's military messages, helping them to win the war.

Sometimes codes look more important than they really are. In 1953, during the Cold War, a coin was found in New York. Inside it there was a coded message, on a tiny piece of micro-film. Four years later, after much hard work, the code was cracked. The secret message was just a note to welcome a new spy from Russia!

Chapter 5
Code Breakers

Now that we had a real reason to crack the code, we could focus our minds on what we had to do. Up in Jack's room, we put the messages out on his bed. There were four text messages – three short ones and a longer one. Jack had written each message on a separate piece of paper, in neat, capital letters:

NLGQD SVRQ RIPR UJDQ

DPEX VKFD URQV FKRR OUXQ

RQHP LOOL RQSR XQGV UDQ VRP

AETHR GDYGD OCGFN KXCGM
FEFTI MGDOY AXDM GQQM GKNQ

We stared at them for a moment or two in silence. Jack spoke first.

"I can't see any repeated letter patterns," he said. "So each word of the secret message looks as if it's only been used once."

"That will make the code harder to crack," I said, with a sigh.

"What kind of code could it be?" I asked. "I know there are different sorts, but my mind's gone blank." Jack sighed and threw me our Code Hand-book.

"Take another look at this then," he said. "I'm going to start by writing the messages out backwards." While Jack did this, I turned to the best part of the hand-book.

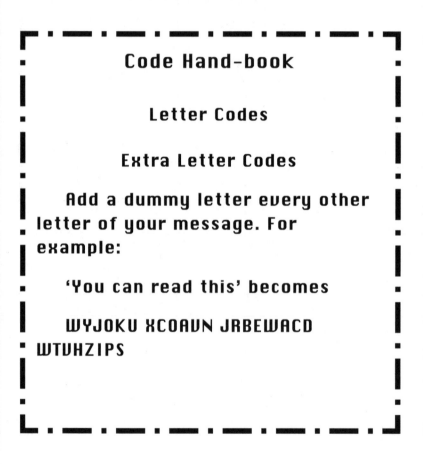

Code Hand-book

Letter Codes

Extra Letter Codes

Add a dummy letter every other letter of your message. For example:

'You can read this' becomes

WYJOKU XCOAVN JRBEWACD WTVHZIPS

Anagram Codes

Write the letters of your message in a different order to make new words. For example:

'You can read this' becomes

A DANCER HITS YOU

There was more of this, but I had enough to be getting on with. Looking at the coded texts, I tried to remove some of the letters, to see if the words made sense without them. When this didn't work, I began swapping the letters round, trying to make anagrams of the messages. After a while, all the letters began to look the same. I was getting nowhere, fast.

"That's it!" cried Jack suddenly, making me jump. "Why didn't I think of it before?" His eyes lit up with excitement. "It's got to be a shift cipher, you know, the kind of code that shifts the alphabet on a few letters. In a shift cipher, each letter of the secret message is replaced by a letter that comes later in the alphabet."

He opened a drawer in his desk and pulled out a small object made of cardboard. He waved it in the air.

"We'll need our cipher disk to crack this code."

I had forgotten all about the cipher disk, but we had often used it to invent our own codes.

"We need to turn the inner disk a few places to the right or left, to see if it makes sense of the letters in our codes," continued Jack. "We could start with the 'shift-3' cipher, where the letter A is shifted along three places to become the letter D."

"Julius Caesar used a code like that!" I said. "I read about it on the Internet."

"If it was good enough for a Roman emperor, then it's good enough for us!" replied Jack.

We tried the 'shift-3' cipher on our text messages, and we were amazed to find it worked. Now we could understand the first three messages:

NLGQD SVRQ RIPR UJDQ

KIDNA   PSON   OFMO RGAN
(kidnap son of Morgan)

DPEX VKFD URQV FKRR OUXQ

AMBU   SHCA   RONS   CHOO   LRUN
(ambush car on school run)

RQHP LOOL RQSR XQGV UDQ VRP

ONEM ILLI   ONPO   UNDS RAN SOM
(one million pounds ransom)

"Who's 'Morgan'?" asked Jack.

"That must be Guy Morgan, the
footballer," I replied. "He lives about two
miles away, in that big house on the hill. You
know the house, it's on the road out of town."

Jack nodded slowly. "You're right," he
said. "His son goes to a private school in

Cambridge. I've heard that Morgan's driver takes him there every day."

The truth was sinking in. We looked at each other.

"This is serious," Jack said. "That man and his gang are plotting to kidnap the boy on his way to school."

"But when are they going to do it?" I asked. "And where?"

"We don't know yet," replied Jack. "Perhaps that's what the fourth message says." He bit his lip. "The only problem is, we can't use the cipher disk on that last message. It's in a different code. I've an awful feeling it's going to be a lot harder to crack."

Chapter 6
First Light

Jack was right about the second code. Three hours later, we were no closer to cracking it. The fourth text was still just a string of letters that meant nothing to us.

In the end, we got so tired that we began to argue. Jack wanted to carry on until we had broken the code, but I didn't agree.

"What if the kidnap is planned for today?" I asked. "We need to go and warn that footballer what's going to happen to his son."

"Do you really think he'd believe us?" snorted Jack. "It's more likely he'd just think we were mad fans. He'd phone for the police alright, but to arrest us, not the kidnappers."

"We could try to warn his son, then," I replied. "We've got to do *something*." Outside Jack's window, a bird began to sing. Soon it would be morning.

"I've got to go home before it gets light," I said. "Mum will kill me if she finds out I've been out all night."

"Your call," muttered Jack, turning his back on me. "Go home to Mummy. Just leave all this to me."

"Don't be stupid," I said, getting angry. "Before I do anything else I'm going to ride to

Morgan's house, to make contact with the kid. Meanwhile, you can carry on cracking the code. Let's hope at least one of us has some success."

Jack turned round to face me. He looked pale from lack of sleep.

"Maybe you're right," he said, rubbing his eyes. "It's true we don't know how long we've got. The kidnap could happen at any time, and that boy's in danger. We'd better split now. But phone me to let me know how you get on."

****

Back outside, the cold night air cleared my mind. I jumped on my bike and rode the two miles to Morgan's house. The footballer's huge mansion was built on top of a hill, like a castle. It was lit up with spot-lights. There was a security fence all around the grounds, with signs telling me to 'Beware of the Dogs'. A small wood lay between the fence and the house.

I've always been good at climbing, so scaling the fence wasn't a problem. The dogs, if there were any, were asleep, and the place was silent. Every move I made seemed to shatter the stillness, like a shot from a gun.

I crept through the woods up to the house. There were no signs of life, and for a few seconds I couldn't tell if the house was empty. Perhaps Morgan was away, and had taken his family with him. But then, a sound came from the house – the distant flush of a toilet. A light went on in one of the upstairs rooms.

I looked up at the window. The light behind the curtains showed the outlines of big stickers on the glass. It was a child's bedroom. I bent down to pick up a small stone, and threw it up against the window. Holding my breath, I waited. Nothing happened, so I threw another stone, harder this time.

There was a twitch of the curtains, and then they opened. A small boy stared out into the darkness.

Code Hand-book

Clever Codes

Make a code by writing your plaintext in zig zag, for example:

'this is a crazy code' becomes

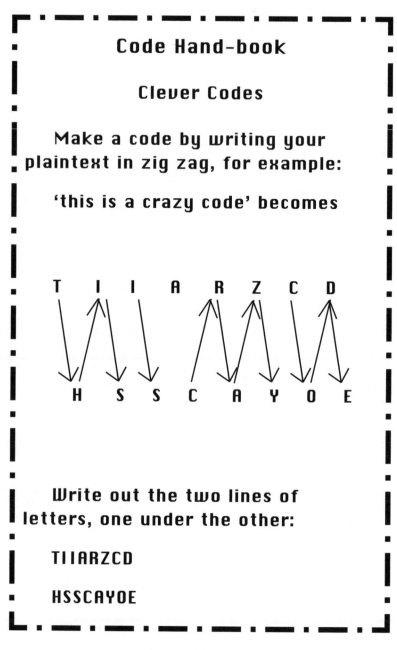

Write out the two lines of letters, one under the other:

TIIARZCD

HSSCAYOE

Now group the letters together
to make your coded message:

TIIA RZCD HSSC AYOE

To decode this message:

1   Count the number of letters
(16). This means each line of the zig
zag message has 8 letters.

2   Write the first 8 letters of the
code in a line above the second 8
letters.

3   To understand the message,
read the letters in a zig zag
direction (down, up, down, up etc.)

Chapter 7
Tall Tales

I stepped out from the shadows. It was important not to scare the boy, so I smiled and waved at him. He waved back. He looked about seven years old.

"Open the window," I mouthed, pointing to the window lock. He did as I asked.

"Who are you?" he called out, in a loud voice. "And what do you want?"

Worried that he was going to wake up his parents, or even worse the guard dogs, I put a finger to my lips.

"Sshhh!" I said. "You don't need to shout. My name's Harry – what's yours?"

"Lee," he replied, in a small voice. "But what are you doing here?"

"Listen, Lee," I said. "I've come to help you. I've got to tell you something really important. I'm telling you, because I know you'll believe me, but I'm not sure your parents will."

This seemed to impress the boy, and his face relaxed into a smile.

"Try me," he said. I took a deep breath.

"You mustn't go to school this morning, Lee," I said. "Think of any excuse, tell your mum that you're feeling sick or something."

"If you say so!" said Lee, now with a broad grin on his face. I could see he liked the idea of missing school. "But why should I do *that*?"

"You're in danger, Lee," I explained, as gently as I could, so as not to alarm him. "Some bad people want to kidnap you. Perhaps today."

Lee's smile vanished.

"How do you know?" he whispered.

"Lee, I can't go into details. It's complicated," I said. That was one way of putting it.

"Why can't I just tell my mum the truth?" he asked, beginning to sound scared.

"She won't believe you," I replied. "Adults don't always believe it when children tell the truth."

"I reckon you're right," said Lee. "But I believe you." He sounded like a bright kid.

"If you tell your mum what I've told you and she thinks you're making it up, then she'll make you go to school," I said. "And that's the last thing you should do today."

Suddenly, Lee turned away from the window. Someone had come into his bedroom.

"Lee? Who are you talking to?" It was a woman's voice.

I stepped back into the darkness, straining to hear what they were saying.

"No one, Mum," came Lee's reply. "I was just opening the window to get some fresh air."

"I'm sure I heard something," said his mum.

"There's no one here," replied Lee. I held my breath.

"Mum, I had a bad night's sleep. I don't feel very well."

A tall figure walked towards the window and pulled the curtains shut. The voices became muffled, and I couldn't hear what they said next. Did Lee's mum believe his story? Would she let him stay at home that morning? I could only hope – there was nothing more I could do now.

I looked down at my watch – it was 6.15am. Time to phone Jack.

I got out my mobile.

"Any luck with the code?" I asked when Jack picked up.

"No," he replied. "Come back and help me, Harry. I feel like my brain's about to explode."

"I'm on my way," I replied. "We've *got* to decode that last message, Jack. If we don't, they're going to win. They're going to kidnap the boy."

For some reason, Jack began to laugh.

"Thanks, Harry!" he said. "You've just given me an idea."

Then he hung up before I could reply, for the second time that night.

Code Hand-book

Difficult Codes

Some codes are so difficult, they are never cracked.

In 1648, King Charles I was put in prison in a castle on the Isle of Wight. He plotted an escape, and sent out messages in a code that used numbers instead of words. The king's plan failed, and a year later he was put to death in London. He was beheaded. The king's code was never cracked, and even today, no one knows what the doomed king wrote from his lonely prison cell.

Chapter 8
The Last Text

As I made my way back through the grounds of the big house, the first rays of light were bringing colour and shape to the new day. I couldn't go home yet – there was still too much to do. But I would have to let Mum know I was OK.

When I reached my bike, I sent Mum a text message, saying I'd gone to do Jack's paper round for him. It would buy me some extra time, so I could go back to help Jack with the code.

A few moments after I had sent this text, my phone rang. For a second I panicked, thinking it was Mum, but it was Jack.

"I've done it!" he said.

"You mean you've cracked it?"

"You're talking to a genius!" he said. "And believe it or not, you helped me break the code, without even knowing it!"

"That makes me a genius too, then," I laughed. "But what do you mean, I helped you?"

"I was looking for a key to the code, and knew it was likely to be a simple, short sentence," said Jack. "The letters of this sentence would replace the first letters of

the alphabet, and then the rest of the alphabet would follow in order."

Jack was talking very fast, and I couldn't keep up.

"Just write it down in our Code Handbook," I said. "And I'm sure it will make sense when I read it."

"Don't worry, I will," said Jack. "This code's a classic!"

"What did I say to you that gave you the key?" I asked. I really had no idea.

"It was the last thing you said when you phoned," replied Jack. "Just three words: 'Kidnap the boy'. I tried this out as the key, and it worked!"

"Well then, tell me!" I said. "What does that last text message say?"

"It says: 'Eight o' clock Monday morning, Brockley Crossroads'," replied Jack with pride. I gasped.

"You know what that means, don't you?" I said, my heart thumping. "That crossroads is just up the road from where I am now." I checked my watch.

"It's already 6.45am. The kidnap is planned for just over an hour's time."

Jack whistled.

"Did you speak to the boy up at the house?"

"Yes, and I don't know if he's going to school today or not," I replied. "He's trying to get out of it, but he might not have much luck. He could be passing Brockley Crossroads in about an hour, on his way to school." As I said this, I made up my mind. For once, Jack wasn't going to change it for me. Lee Morgan was just a kid, and he was in real danger.

"I'm sorry Jack, but we can't risk it. We've got to go to the police now."

This time, Jack didn't argue.

"You're right," he said. "We can't deal with this on our own any more. You'd better ride straight to the police station. I'll meet you there."

Code Hand-book

Key Word Codes

This kind of code uses a secret key word or short sentence that is only known by people using the code. The letters of the key words replace the first letters of the alphabet.

For example, if the key words are 'Kidnap the boy', then these letters form the first 12 letters of the codetext alphabet:

a	b	c	d	e	f	g	h	h	j	k	l
K	I	D	N	A	P	T	H	E	B	O	Y

The rest of the alphabet follows in alphabetical order, missing out any letters that have already been used:

m	n	o	p	q	r	s	t	u	v	w	x	y	z
C	F	G	J	L	M	Q	R	S	U	V	W	X	Z

The complete codetext alphabet is as follows:

a	b	c	d	e	f	g	h	i	j	k	l	m	n	o	p	q	r	s	t	u	v	w	q	y	z
K	I	D	N	A	P	T	H	E	B	O	Y	C	F	G	J	L	M	Q	R	S	U	V	W	X	Z

So, using 'KIDNAP THE BOY' as a secret key, the plaintext message:

Eight o clock Monday morning Brockley Crossroads

becomes:

AETHR GDYGD OCGFN KXCGM
FEFTI MGDOY AXDM GQQM GKNQ

Chapter 9
Missing Proof

The sun was rising in the sky, and the world was waking up. As I rode past the train station, people were beginning their journey to work. It was hard to believe that only yesterday, Jack and I had begun our adventure in that place. It felt like a year had passed since then.

My thoughts were racing. What if Lee Morgan went to school that morning after all? And what if the police didn't believe our story? After all, we didn't really have much proof to back it up – the kidnappers had the mobile phone, and all we had were a few scraps of paper covered in letters and scribbles. I was struck by a horrible thought. If Lee Morgan *was* kidnapped that morning, he might tell his kidnappers we had warned him about the plot. They knew where we lived ...

I arrived at the police station, hot and out of breath. Jack was waiting there for me, a huge grin on his face. He didn't seem worried at all.

"It's all here," he called out cheerfully. He waved a plastic bag in the air.

"I've written out the codes. Let's go inside!"

I followed him through the swing doors, feeling nervous enough for both of us.

"Can I help you, lads?" asked the young police officer on duty at the front desk. He looked friendly, so I spoke up.

"Yes, please, we want to report a crime," I said.

"But it hasn't happened yet," Jack chipped in. I aimed a sharp kick at his shin – I had a feeling that it would be better if I did the talking.

"There's a plot to kidnap the son of Guy Morgan, the footballer," I explained. I went on to describe the events of the last 24 hours. The police officer let me talk. He frowned as he listened. When I had finished, he asked to see the codes, so Jack fished them out of his bag. The police officer looked at them in silence.

"Excuse me, lads," he said. "I'll just have a word with the boss. Sit down."

Ten minutes later, the police officer returned with an older man in a plain suit. The senior officer introduced himself.

"My name's Paxton, and I'm a detective inspector," he said. "I'd like you both to come with me to answer some questions."

He looked at us over the top of his glasses. "I hope for your sake that you are not wasting police time."

"You've got to believe us!" I cried, I felt desperate. "It's half past seven. Only thirty minutes to go before the kidnap!"

Detective Inspector Paxton checked his watch.

"It's a quiet morning," he said to the younger officer. "We might as well send two patrol cars to check out that crossroads. It looks like a school-boy prank, but it's better to be safe than sorry."

Jack and I looked at each other. It was clear the police didn't really believe us, but that didn't matter now. The patrol cars were on their way to Brockley Crossroads, where the police would see the truth for themselves.

Code Hand-book

Cracking Codes

When a code is cracked, it's normally bad news for the code maker.

In 1587, Queen Elizabeth I sent her cousin Mary Queen of Scots to prison, because she didn't want her to become Queen of England. Mary plotted to kill Elizabeth from her prison cell. Mary sent out coded messages, which fell into the wrong hands. The codes were cracked and Mary was beheaded.

Chapter 10
Important Visitors

Detective Inspector Paxton showed us into an interview room.

"WPC Green will sit with you here, while we find some forms for you to fill in," he said. With that, he stepped out of the room, leaving us with a plump, bitter-looking woman. She pointed to some hard plastic chairs lined up against the wall, and we sat down.

"Do your parents know you are here?" she asked. We looked at each other. For some reason, we hadn't counted on this.

"Not exactly," I said.

"We will need to inform them," she replied coldly.

As she took down our phone numbers, it felt like we were the ones who were in trouble. I tried not to think about what my Mum would do when she had a phone call from the police station.

The paper-work seemed to take a long time. My thoughts turned to Lee – where was he now? Had the police got to the Crossroads in time? As if he had been reading my mind, Detective Inspector Paxton came into the room.

"It seems your information was correct," he said, with a look of surprise. "We have just made a number of arrests, and a serious crime has been prevented."

"Is Lee OK?" I asked quickly.

"Lee Morgan was not present at the scene. We have spoken to his parents. He is sick, and hasn't gone to school today." I smiled to myself.

"Did you get the kidnappers' mobile phones?" Jack asked.

"Indeed we did," replied Paxton. "The coded text messages were still on them, giving us the proof we needed to arrest the gang."

The police officer from the front desk put his head round the door.

"Sir, we have some rather important visitors," he said. "They'd like to speak to the boys."

Guy Morgan walked into the room with Lee, who caught my eye and grinned.

"We came here as soon as we heard from the police, and Lee explained about your early morning visit," the famous footballer said. Jack and I stared at him. He looked even taller in real life than he did on 'Match of the Day.'

Morgan put his arm around his son.

"Well, boys," he said. "I'd like to thank you for what you've done. Now that I don't have to pay a ransom to those kidnappers, I've got some spare cash to give away."

With that, he handed each of us a big wad of bank notes.

"And I want you to come with me to watch Dad play football," said Lee. "So Dad's going to get you some season tickets for his Premier League Club."

Too stunned to reply, Jack and I just stood there, with our mouths open. Then my mum burst into the room. "Don't forget to say thank you!" she said. Jack's mum was following close behind.

"I *should* ground you for staying out all night," Mum said. "But I've been told you've done something useful, for once."

"You're quite right," laughed Morgan. "You should be proud of these boys. They're real heroes."

****

The news of the kidnap plot soon broke to the media. The next day, Jack and I were on the front pages of all the papers. It's a big story, so the phone hasn't stopped ringing all week. Reporters are still asking us for interviews.

It's a good job Mum is happy to answer the calls for me. I'm much too busy playing with my brand new mobile phone. Jack's got one too – we bought them with our reward money. We're having lots of fun texting each other, trying out new codes.

****

As I finish writing my blog, I can see how things could have ended in a very different way for Jack and me. We cracked the code, so everything worked out well for us, but what if we hadn't found the missing key? Code breaking is risky, and whatever happens, it can change your life forever.

AUTHOR FACT FILE
DEBORAH CHANCELLOR

What would your code name be if you were a secret agent?
I would take the code name 'Kingfisher', a bird that is rare and hard to spot. They are so quick, all you see is a flash, and then they're gone.

Tell us some TOP SECRET info about you.
I can use my left hand as well as my right to do most things. This can come in useful when I want to cut my finger-nails in a hurry!

What inspired you to write this book?
I have been interested in codes, and the people who crack them, for as long as I can remember. I wondered what it would be like to try to break a code, if it was a matter of life or death. This gave me the idea for my story.

What is your favourite type of code? And why?
I like the idea of a code that is so complex, no one in the world can solve it. There is a document called the Voynich manuscript, which was written in code about 800 years ago. No one has ever been able to decode it. Anyone who manages to crack this code today will become a famous code breaking celebrity! To see some pages of the document, go to www.voynich.nu.

ILLUSTRATOR FACT FILE
ZOOGRAFIC

What would your code name be if you were a secret agent?

Tell us some TOP SECRET info about you.

How would you hide a code?

If you were given reward money like Jack and Harry what would you spend it on?

Barrington Stoke would like to thank all its readers for commenting on the manuscript before publication and in particular:

Joe Brown
Matthew Bumby
Helen Cox
James Cox
Harry Curtis
Helen Degazon
Sean Deere
F. Devereux
Ryan Diuga
Tristan Eyre
Jenny Linsley
April Pearson
Becky Russell
Josh Scott
Tom Scurr
Declan Suddaby

Become a Consultant!

Would you like to give us feedback on our titles before they are published? Contact us at the email address below – we'd love to hear from you!

info@barringtonstoke.co.uk
www.barringtonstoke.co.uk